Julia Donaldson   Yuval Zommer

The
WOOLLY BEAR
CATERPILLAR

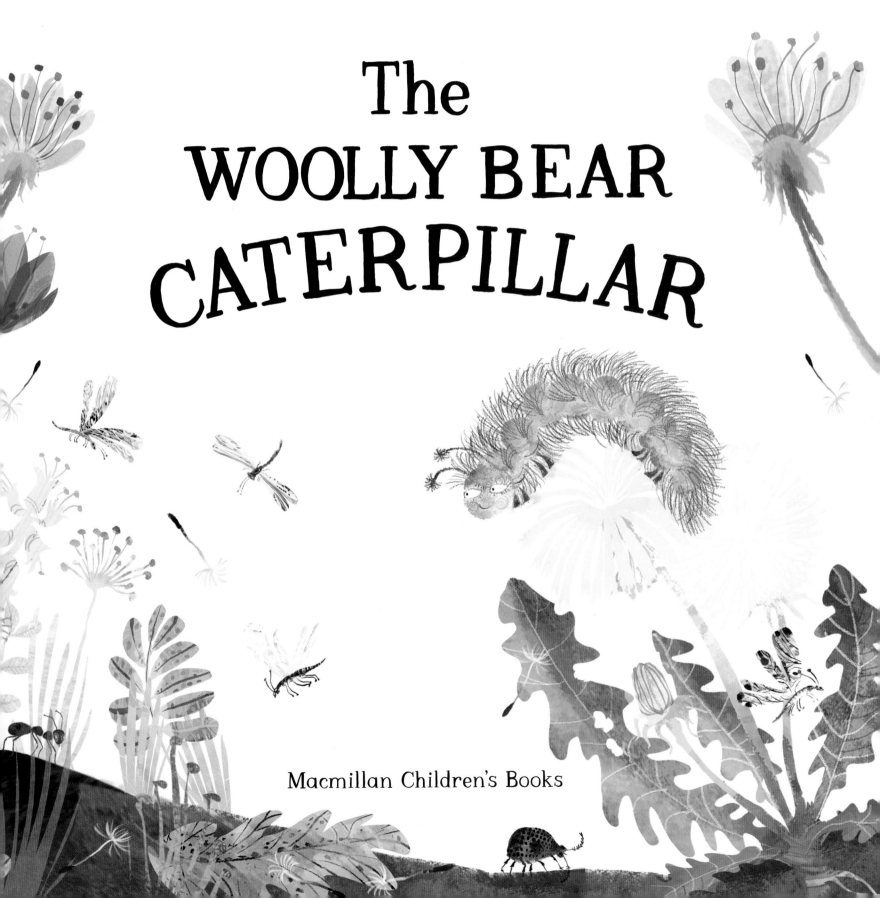

Macmillan Children's Books

There was once a woolly bear caterpillar. She lived in a garden and she loved eating dandelion leaves.

But one day, a gardener
pulled up all the dandelions
in the flower bed.

The woolly bear caterpillar had to
crawl off in search of some new ones.

She hadn't crawled far when she heard someone singing. On a leaf of a sycamore tree sat a caterpillar with very long yellow and orange hair, and this was her song . . .

"Look at me!
Look at me!
I'm bonny and bright as can be.
With my hair of bright gold,
I'm a joy to behold,
The queen of the sycamore tree."

"Hello. What's your name?" asked the woolly bear caterpillar. "I'm a sycamore caterpillar, and I'm going to turn into a sycamore moth. Just think – if I'm so pretty now, I'll be absolutely gorgeous when I get my wings."

"I'm going to have wings too one day," said the woolly bear caterpillar.

The sycamore caterpillar laughed. "Yes, very plain ones, I expect. Never mind, we can't all be beautiful."

The woolly bear caterpillar crawled
on till she reached an apple tree.
On a fallen apple sat a caterpillar with
red spots and bright yellow tufts.
He was singing this song . . .

"Look at me!
Look at me!
I'm stunning and smart as can be.
With my tufts of bright yellow,
    I'm such a fine fellow,
The king of the old apple tree."

"Hello. What's your name?" asked the woolly bear caterpillar.
"I'm a vapourer caterpillar. I'm good-looking, aren't I?
And I'll be even more handsome when I'm a moth."

"I'll be a moth too one day,"
said the woolly bear caterpillar.

The vapourer caterpillar laughed.
"Yes, a very dull one, I imagine.
Never mind, we can't all be colourful."

The woolly bear caterpillar crawled on till she came to a tall poplar tree. On a twig was a very strange-looking caterpillar.

He was bright green, and round his head were some red marks that made it look as if he was screaming. He was singing this song . . .

"Look at me!
Look at me!
I'm stunning and strange as can be.
The marks round my head
Are a fierce fiery red.
I'm the king of the tall poplar tree."

"Hello. What's your name?" asked the woolly bear caterpillar. "I'm a puss moth caterpillar. Don't I look weird and wonderful? And if I'm so unusual now, just think how extraordinary I'll be when I become a moth."

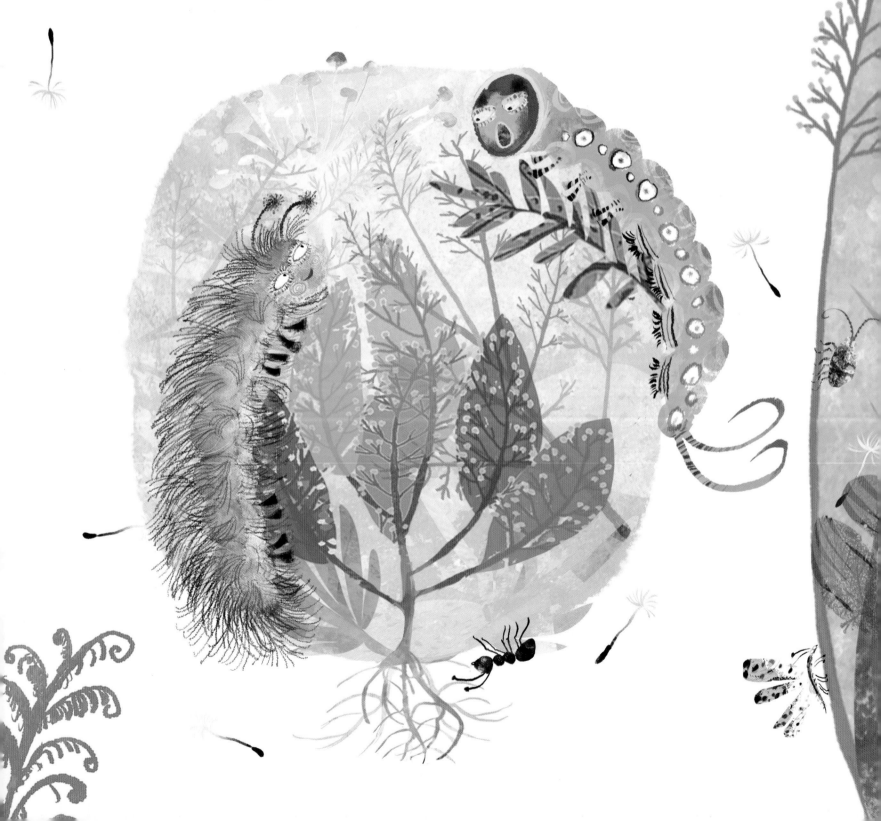

"I wonder what sort of moth I'll become," said the woolly bear caterpillar.

The puss moth caterpillar laughed.
"A very boring one, I should think," he said.
"Never mind, we can't all be perfect."

The woolly bear caterpillar felt a little sad.
She wished she could be beautiful and exciting
instead of plain and dull. But then at last she
found some dandelion leaves, which cheered her up.

After a tasty meal, she crawled under a big dock leaf. "It's time I got ready to change into a moth," she decided, and she started to spin herself a nice silky coat called a cocoon.

The sycamore caterpillar was spinning a cocoon too, in some old leaves on the ground.

The vapourer caterpillar's cocoon was on a twig of the apple tree.

And the puss moth caterpillar had found a snug hole in the poplar tree's bark for his cocoon.

Weeks went by. Then it was time for the moths to hatch out of their cocoons.

Out hatched the sycamore moth. She looked quite plain.

Out hatched the vapourer
moth. He looked rather
dull. He did have two white
spots on his wings but they
weren't very exciting.

Out hatched the puss moth.
He looked fairly boring,
even though his wings did
have a few squiggles.

The three moths flew round the garden.

"Let's see if Woolly Bear has hatched out yet," said Sycamore.

"Good idea – at least she'll look more ordinary than us," said Vapourer.

"Look, here's her cocoon," said Puss Moth. The three of them settled on the grass to watch. They didn't have long to wait.

The cocoon split open,
and out hatched . . .

a lovely orange, black and white
moth. She had splendid blue spots,
and her body was stripy like a tiger.

"She's beautiful,"
said Sycamore.

"She's colourful,"
said Vapourer.

"She's
perfect,"
said Puss Moth.

"And I'm not a woolly bear any more," said the newly hatched moth. "I'm a **garden tiger moth!**"

And feeling very happy she fluttered into the air.

The other three moths gazed up at her longingly.
Then all together they sang this song . . .

"Look at her!
Way up there!
No longer a small woolly bear.
She's a beautiful sight.
She's a perfect delight,
The colourful queen of the air."

JULIA DONALDSON is the writer of many of the world's best-loved picture books, including *The Gruffalo* and the What the Ladybird Heard adventures. She was Children's Laureate 2011-13, and was awarded a CBE for Services to Literature. Julia and her husband, Malcolm, divide their time between Edinburgh and West Sussex. They love the great outdoors and can often be found walking on the South Downs, identifying plants and minibeasts galore . . . including caterpillars!

© Steve Ullathorne

YUVAL ZOMMER graduated from the Royal College of Art with an MA in Illustration. He worked for many years as a creative director in advertising agencies before turning his hand to writing and illustrating award-winning children's books, focusing on animals and the natural world. Yuval lives and works in an old house in London overlooking a small garden that is visited by foxes, birds, squirrels and many insects, some of which later find their way into his books.

© Ian Hessenberg

For the Sussex Wildlife Trust — JD
To my wonderful niece Noya — YZ

First published 2021 by Macmillan Children's Books
an imprint of Pan Macmillan
The Smithson, 6 Briset Street, London EC1M 5NR
EU representative: Macmillan Publishers Ireland Limited,
Mallard Lodge, Lansdowne Village, Dublin 4
Associated companies throughout the world
www.panmacmillan.com

ISBN: 978-1-5290-1218-7

1 3 5 7 9 8 6 4 2

A CIP catalogue record for this book is available from the British Library.
Printed in China

FSC
www.fsc.org
MIX
Paper from
responsible sources
FSC® C116313